THERE IS NO DRAGON IN THIS STORY

LOU CARTER

DEBORAH ALLWRIGHT

For Pete, Josh and Fee. Obvs. – L.C.

For Lola Carlotta – D.A.

Bloomsbury Publishing, London, Oxford, New York, New Delhi and Sydney

First published in Great Britain in 2017 by Bloomsbury Publishing Plc
50 Bedford Square, London WC1B 3DP

www.bloomsbury.com

BLOOMSBURY is a registered trademark of Bloomsbury Publishing Plc

Text copyright © Lou Carter 2017
Illustrations copyright © Deborah Allwright 2017

The moral rights of the author and illustrator have been asserted

A CIP catalogue record of this book is available from the British Library

ISBN 978 1 4088 6489 0 (HB)
ISBN 978 1 4088 6490 6 (PB)
ISBN 978 1 4088 6488 3 (eBook)

All papers used by Bloomsbury Publishing are natural, recyclable products made
from wood grown in well managed forests. The manufacturing processes
conform to the environmental regulations of the country of origin

Printed in China by Leo Paper Products, Heshan, Guangdong

1 3 5 7 9 10 8 6 4 2

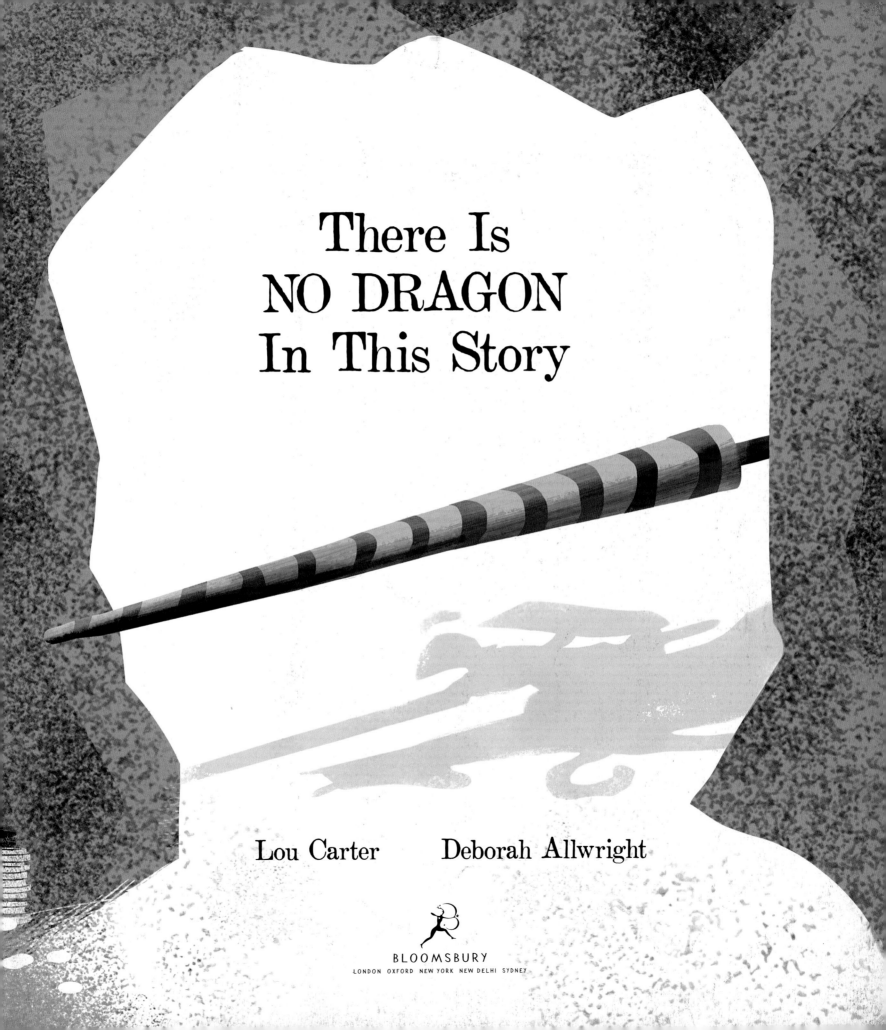

There Is
NO DRAGON
In This Story

Lou Carter   Deborah Allwright

BLOOMSBURY
LONDON OXFORD NEW YORK NEW DELHI SYDNEY

This was supposed to be a story about a dragon

BOOO-HISS!

who captured a princess

OH NO!

when . . .

SCREAM!

... Along came a knight

YAY!

who fought with the dragon

GASP!

and rescued the princess.

HURRAH!

The end.

However, I can't tell you that story because Dragon has gone off in a huff.

I will not capture any icky, frilly
princesses today. And I shall not fight
any more brave, shiny knights.
I'm going to a story where
I can be the HERO for a change!

First, Dragon sees a little biscuit man.

Hello! Can I be in your story? I could save you from that Fox!

"No, no, no, that's not how it goes," says the Gingerbread Man. "There is NO DRAGON in this story."

Next, Dragon climbs the hill where he meets a pig building a house out of sticks.

Hello! Can I be in your story? I could save you from that Big Bad Wolf!

"No, no, no, that's not how it goes," says the Second Little Pig. "There is NO DRAGON in this story."

So, Dragon sets off towards the town.

On the way he tries
to help Goldilocks . . .

NO!

THIS WAY

NO!

NO!

And Hansel and Gretel . . .

NO!

And Little Red Riding Hood.

THAT WAY

But nobody wants Dragon in their story.

But, hang on, Dragon
has spotted a boy
climbing a beanstalk.

Hello! I could save you
from the Giant.

"No, no, no, that's not how it goes," says Jack. "There is NO DRAGON in this story."

Boy oh boy, what is happening here?

THERE!

HERE

Give us a kiss!

Move over!

"DRAGON ... where are you?"
shouts the Gingerbread Man.
"What we need is a hero!"

I can't. I'm no good at hero-ing.

"But we really need a
DRAGON in this story!"
says the Gingerbread Man.

I can't . . .

Can I?

Can I?!

I CAN!

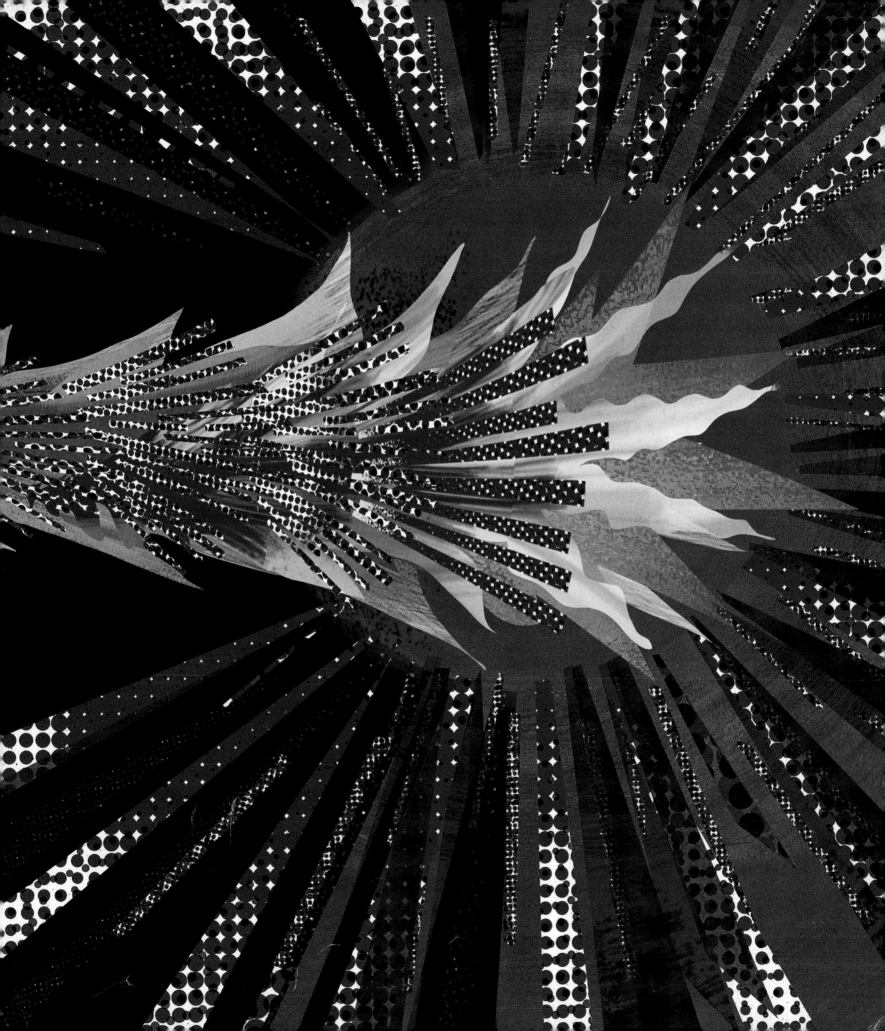

HURRAH!

A hero at last!

HURRAH!

So there you have it: a story about a brave dragon

BOOO-HISS!

who makes the Giant sneeze

OH NO!

and out goes the sun . . .

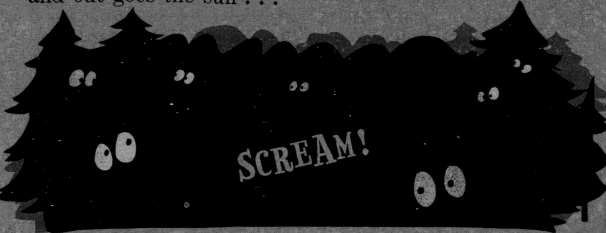

SCREAM!

. . . But Dragon makes it light again

YAY!

and is a HERO!

HURRAH!

The end.

Hang on! Where's Dragon gone now?